MW00800053

Chrissy Cottontail

Dave and Pat Sargent are longtime residents of Prairie Grove, Arkansas. Dave, a fourth-generation dairy farmer, began writing in early December of 1990, and Pat, a former teacher, began writing in the fourth grade. They enjoy the outdoors and have a real love for animals.

Chrissy Cottontail

Animal Pride Series
Book 7

By

Dave and Pat Sargent

Beyond The End
By
Sue Rogers

Illustrated by
Jeane Lirley Huff

Ozark Publishing, Inc.
P.O. Box 228
Prairie Grove, AR 72753

Cataloging-in-publication data

Sargent, Dave, 1941-
   Chrissy Cottontail / by Dave and Pat Sargent ; illustrated by Jeane Lirley Huff. —Prairie Grove, AR :
Ozark Publishing, ©2003.
   ix, 36 p. : col. ill. ; 21 cm.   (Animal pride series ; 7)
   "Mind your mama"—Cover.
   SUMMARY: Young Chrissy sits on the high bank
and watches the hounds below. When ole hound dog
named Barney gets a whiff of the rabbit, he takes off
after her. Includes facts about the physical characteris-
tics, behavior, habitat, and predators of the rabbit.
   ISBN: 1-56763-771-X (hc)
          1-56763-772-8 (pbk)
      1. Cottontails—Juvenile fiction. [1. Cottontails—
Fiction. 2. Rabbits—Fiction] I. Sargent, Pat, 1936-
II. Huff, Jeane Lirley, 1946- ill. III. Title. IV. Series:
Sargent, Dave, 1941- Animal pride series ; 7.

   PZ10.3.S243Ch 2003
   [Fic]—dc21   96-001494

Factual information excerpted/adapted from
THE WORLD BOOK ENCYCLOPEDIA.
© World Book, Inc. By permission of the publisher.
www.worldbook.com

Printed in the United States of America

iv

Inspired by

watching fast frisky little cottontails play.

Dedicated to

Barney the Bear Killer, Pat's friend.

Foreword

Chrissy was not supposed to play so far from home. She was supposed to stay close to her sister and brothers. But one day while she was out exploring the woods, she got too close to a coonhound named Barney. When Ole Barney got a whiff of rabbit, he took off after her! If only little Chrissy had minded her mama.

Contents

One   Chrissy's Narrow Escape   1

Two   The Trap   11

Three   Ole Barney's "Gotcha" Howl!   17

Four   Rabbit Facts   27

If you would like to have the authors of the Animal Pride Series visit your school, free of charge, call 1-800-321-5671 or 1-800-960-3876.

One

Chrissy's Narrow Escape

Chrissy sat on the high bank of the creek and watched the hounds below. They were running up and down the creek bed trying to pick up her trail. Chrissy knew that if she moved, even the slightest little bit, the hounds would be on her like syrup on pancakes.

One of the coonhounds spotted Chrissy. It lifted its head and let out a long bay. She recognized the hound by the deep scars on his left side. It was the one her brothers referred to as Barney the Bear Killer. He had earned the name by killing a mean ole grizzly bear that had been killing Farmer John's calves.

Ole Barney's nose was on the ground and Chrissy just knew that he had picked up her scent. She sat there trembling with fear, trying to decide what to do. She waited until Barney turned his nose away from her, then, quick as a flash, she shot through the blackberry bushes and into Farmer John's cotton patch.

Chrissy ran between the rows of cotton. She stopped half-way through the cotton patch and crawled under one of the cotton plants. It was autumn in Arkansas and all the cotton bolls were fully open. On the end of every stem was an open boll with fluffy balls of white cotton just waiting to be picked. Chrissy sat under one of these plants with her head down low and her white cotton tail sticking up close to some of the fluffy white cotton. She thought, "If Barney the Bear Killer comes down this row, maybe he'll think my little white cotton tail is just a white ball of cotton on this cotton plant."

In all the excitement, Chrissy forgot what her mama had told her and her brothers and sister. Then suddenly, she remembered her mama saying, "Now, children, remember that a dog uses his nose as well as his eyes when hunting for food, so always stay upwind from him."

Chrissy tried to think. She closed her eyes, and if rabbits pray, she probably prayed, "Dear God, don't let Barney the Bear Killer eat me!"

Just then, she heard a familiar sound coming from a few feet away. She opened her eyes, and two rows over were two of her brothers. They were the fastest bunnies in the whole wide world—well, at least in their part of Arkansas. They wiggled their noses and winked one eye, and tossed their heads to the right.

Chrissy was a smart little bunny and quickly understood. She had watched them pull this trick before.

The sounds of the hounds drew nearer, and just as Chrissy got set to dart to her right, Barney the Bear Killer came thrashing through the cotton patch. Chrissy's heart was beating fast, and her legs got weak. She was so scared she almost forgot the plan.

Barney the Bear Killer let out a "gotcha" howl when he spotted little Chrissy under the cotton plant.

Chrissy Cottontail tightened her muscles in her tiny legs, and just as Barney the Bear Killer reached her, she made a fast dash to the right. Her brothers, Jack and Mack, the fastest little rabbits in Arkansas, cut between her and Ole Barney. When Barney the Bear Killer saw them flash by, he thought, "Aha! Two rabbits are better than one." He took off after them instead of Chrissy.

Chrissy Cottontail ran as fast as she could in the direction of home, yelling, "Mama! Help me, Mama! Barney the Bear Killer's after me!"

Mama Rabbit rushed out of the thicket, then stepped aside when she saw little Chrissy coming. Chrissy ran into the thicket and to her corner. She fell onto her bed with her heart going thumpity, thump, thump, thump in her chest. It was hard for her to believe that she was safe. She had really thought that Ole Barney was going to eat her!

Chrissy's mama waited for her to calm down, then asked, "What's wrong, Chrissy? Was something after you?" Chrissy nodded.

Mama Rabbit said, "Chrissy, I hope you've learned a lesson. I've told you over and over that you should not go out alone. Now, promise me that you'll stay close to your brothers and sister when you are out playing."

"I promise, Mama," Chrissy said.

Suddenly, Chrissy remembered her brothers and her heart started racing again. She said, "Mama, Jack and Mack saved my life. I hope they're all right. I hope Ole Barney didn't catch them." Mama Rabbit smiled.

Chrissy Cottontail's bed was made of grass and leaves. She laid there thinking about her sister and her brothers. All the little bunnies had brown eyes that twinkled when they were happy and little black noses that wiggled most of the time, especially when their mama and daddy led them into Farmer John's garden.

An hour had passed before Jack and Mack got home. Chrissy and the other bunnies were waiting just outside the berry thicket watching for them. When Chrissy saw that they were safe, she hopped up and down and the two brothers knew that she was glad to see them.

Chrissy said, "Oh, thank you for leading Barney the Bear Killer away from me! I'm ever so grateful! Did he almost catch you? I just know he did! I just know he almost caught you!"

The two brothers smiled and wiggled their noses. They were pleased that Chrissy was grateful to them for saving her life.

Two

The Trap

Early the next morning, before the eastern sky was light, Chrissy's mama and daddy took the bunnies out for breakfast. Chrissy's mama never had to cook breakfast or lunch or supper.

Chrissy and her family went to Farmer John's garden for breakfast. They had breakfast there most of the time. Farmer John's garden was the only garden for miles. Of course, in the wintertime, the rabbits had to eat certain roots, bark, and sometimes berries, because Farmer John did not have a winter garden. The weather in Arkansas was too cold.

When the rabbit family got to the garden fence, they stopped and looked all around. Father Rabbit made sure that they approached the garden downwind from Ole Barney. Chrissy was glad that her father was being cautious, because she didn't want that ole coonhound to get after her again.

Chrissy stood on her back legs and looked toward the barn. Jack and Mack had told her that Barney slept under the side shed that was attached to the barn. The side shed was on the other side of the barn, away from the garden.

Chrissy's family didn't know it, but Farmer John was well aware that rabbits were eating from his garden. And just the night before, he had set a trap in the garden. Chrissy's dad was smart. He knew all about traps. He had learned about traps when he was even younger than Chrissy. His father had been caught in one.

So now, Daddy Rabbit told his family, "Wait here." He started a quick search where the lettuce and cabbage were growing. He would also check the carrot row, because he knew how Chrissy loved carrots. He knew she would head that way.

Chrissy's daddy was right. Her favorite food was tender carrots. She also liked lettuce and most other vegetables. She was hungry and wished Daddy would hurry. Mama was busy watching Jack and Mack, and wasn't watching Chrissy.

Chrissy kept inching closer and closer to the long row of carrots. She thought, "Surely it wouldn't hurt to pull just one little ole carrot before Daddy comes back."

Now, Daddy Rabbit had gone to Chrissy's right when he had begun his search for traps. And Chrissy was inching to her left, into the part of the garden that Daddy Rabbit had not yet checked.

Chrissy spotted a juicy carrot. She could tell by the top of a carrot whether the carrot, growing in the ground, was the right size to eat.

She looked to see where her daddy was. He was searching for traps on the very last row. It was the long row of carrots.

Chrissy thought, "Daddy has not yet found a trap, so maybe

there's not a trap in the garden at all. I'll just pull this one juicy carrot, and no one will know that I didn't wait."

Chrissy reached out and tugged at the carrot, grabbing it just above the ground. It wouldn't budge, so she pulled harder. The tender top broke off in Chrissy's hand and she tumbled backward.

At the exact moment the carrot top broke, causing Chrissy to fall backward. The trap that Farmer John had very carefully placed between that carrot and the one next to it, went off. It made a loud noise!

Everyone in the garden jumped! They headed for the fence as fast as they could run!

Three

Ole Barney's "Gotcha" Howl!

Out under the side shed, Ole Barney the Bear Killer heard the trap go off and thought, "Aha! Sounds like Farmer John caught himself a rabbit. Maybe he'll give me a few bites of it. I love fresh rabbit!"

Barney got up and stretched, then headed for the garden at a trot, thinking, "No use in hurrying. That trap I saw Farmer John set will stop a rabbit cold! I see the back door opening. I guess Farmer John heard the trap, too."

Chrissy and her family were on their way home, running as fast as their legs would go. But they had left the garden so fast they forgot to stay downwind from Barney.

Now Ole Barney the Bear Killer had a keen nose and suddenly picked up the strong scent of rabbit. The scent was not coming from the garden. It was coming from out in the field a ways. He let out a long hound dog bark and headed in the direction of the strong rabbit scent, picking up speed as he ran. Rabbit for breakfast would sure taste good!

Farmer John had now reached the garden. He hurried down the row where he had set the trap. He bent over and pulled the plants apart. The trap had been thrown, but there was nothing in it.

Farmer John scratched his head and said, "Doggone it! I was hoping to have fried rabbit for supper. I guess Molly will have to put on some beans and ham hock instead."

When Farmer John started back toward the house, he saw Ole Barney disappear into the woods and thought, "That fool hound will never catch that rabbit. It has too much of a head start on him. Oh, well, he needs the exercise. I'd better get to the house and tell Molly to get those beans on the stove."

Chrissy's family was ahead of her. They were almost home, and she was bringing up the rear. She heard that old "gotcha" howl from Barney the Bear Killer, and felt his hot breath on her fuzzy white tail. First, she zigzagged left, then right. She was trying to confuse Barney, but it didn't work very well. Barney made a dive for Chrissy Cottontail. She was so frightened she leaped a good ten feet through the air!

When she hit the ground, she swerved to the right, and Barney ran past her. She dived into the thicket and was relieved to see her family crouching there. She froze, sitting completely motionless, hoping to escape Barney.

Chrissy was downwind from Barney and by the time he stopped and turned around, he figured she was long gone. Besides, it was time for him to be getting on back to the house, for he just remembered that Farmer John was going to be moving a few cows to a different pasture today and would need his help.

When Farmer John walked in the back door, a teary-eyed April was waiting. Farmer John stopped, sat down, and pulled her over to him. He asked, "Is that morning dew in your eyes, J.J.? They're wet and shiny like dew on grass."

April sniffed and said, "Daddy, please don't kill the little rabbits. I was watching from my bedroom window, and one of those rabbits was the same little cottontail rabbit that I've played with before. She's a nice little rabbit, Daddy. Her family was with her today. They were probably hungry."

Farmer John said, "I didn't know that the rabbits were your friends, J.J.. So, you know one of them, do you?"

April climbed on Farmer John's knee. She reached up and put her arms around his neck. She kissed him on the cheek and said, "Yes, Daddy. I call that little one, Chrissy. She's a nice little rabbit. When I'm near the edge of the woods on the other side of the garden, she sometimes plays with me."

"And just how do you know that your little friend is a girl, J.J.? Most rabbits look about the same to me," Farmer John said with a smile.

"Because Chrissy is larger than the other baby rabbits. Amber says girl rabbits are larger than boys, so, she must be a girl," reasoned April. Farmer John smiled at April's logic. It did sound reasonable.

Farmer John hugged her tightly and said, "I'll tell you what let's do, J.J.. Let's start plantin' a little extra garden every year for Chrissy and her family so they won't go hungry."

April gave a squeal and clapped her hands together. She said, "Oh, thank you, Daddy! Come on, let's go get that ole trap out of the garden."

So, Chrissy Cottontail and her family soon discovered that no one bothered them when they visited Farmer John's garden. Of course, Daddy Rabbit made sure that they always approached the garden down-wind from Barney. They had really had a close call with that black and tan coonhound, especially Chrissy. It would suit her just fine if she never again came face to face with Barney the Bear Killer.

Four

Rabbit Facts

A rabbit is a furry animal with long ears and a short fluffy tail. They do not walk or run, as most other four-legged animals do. They move about by hopping on their hind legs, which are longer and stronger than their front legs. They also use their front legs when they move. Rabbits balance on their front legs much as people balance on their hands when they play leap frog. When chased by an enemy, a rabbit can hop eighteen miles an hour.

Rabbits live in Africa, Europe, North America, and other parts. They make their homes in fields and prairies where they can hide their young under bushes or in tall grass.

A female carries her young inside her body for twenty-six to thirty days before birth. She has four or five young, called kittens or kits, at a time, but she may have only two or as many as nine. The kits cannot see or hear, and they have no fur. The mother keeps them in a nest she has dug in the ground.

She does not stay in the nest, but remains nearby. She lines the nest and covers the kits with grass and with fur that she pulls from her chest with her teeth. The cover hides the newborn rabbits and keeps them warm. By the time the kits are about ten days old, they can see and hear, and they have a coat of soft fur.

About two weeks after birth, the kits leave the nest and hide in tall grass and leaves. They usually dig their first forms near the nest. The mother seldom feeds her young for more than a few weeks after birth.

Some female cottontails leave to start their own families when less than six months old. A female has four or five young at a time, and may give birth several times a year.

Rabbits in the southern United States, where the weather is warm most of the year, may have babies more than five times a year.

Today, most rabbits used for food and fur are raised by people, but sports enthusiasts still hunt wild rabbits. Many people enjoy rabbit meat, which is sold fresh or frozen.

Rabbit skins are used for making fur coats, or as trimming for cloth coats and hats. The skins can be cut and dyed to look like mink, beaver, or some other more valuable fur. A felt is made by squeezing rabbit fur together with other kinds of fur.

Rabbits and hares look much alike and are often mistaken for each other. Some are even misnamed. For example, the Belgian hare is a rabbit, and the jack rabbit is a hare.

31

Most rabbits are smaller than hares and have shorter ears. The animals can be told apart most easily at birth. A newborn rabbit is blind, it has no fur, and it cannot move about. A newborn hare can see, it has a coat of fine fur, and it can hop a few hours after birth. In addition to that, the bones in a rabbit's skull have a different size and shape from those in a hare's skull.

Rabbits and hares belong to the same order or group of the animal kingdom. The name of this order, Lagomorpha, comes from two Greek words meaning hare-shaped.

Wild rabbits have soft thick brownish or grayish fur. The fur of pet rabbits may be black, brown, gray, white, or combinations of these colors. Adult wild rabbits grow eight to fourteen inches long and weigh two to five pounds. Pet rabbits may grow about eight inches longer and weigh five pounds more. Most female rabbits are larger than males.

Few rabbits live more than a year in the wild because they have little protection against enemies. Many pet rabbits live as long as five years.

A rabbit's eyes are on the sides of its head, so the animal can see things behind or to the side better than in front. Rabbits can move their long ears together or one at a time to catch even faint sounds from any direction. Rabbits also depend on their keen sense of smell to alert them to danger. A rabbit seems to twitch its nose almost all the time.

Rabbits were once classified as rodents (gnawing animals). Like

beavers, mice, and other rodents, rabbits have chisel-like front teeth for gnawing. But unlike rodents, rabbits have a pair of small teeth behind the upper front teeth.

A rabbit's tail is about two inches long and is covered with soft fluffy fur that makes it look round. The fur on the underside of the tail of most kinds of rabbits has a lighter color than that on top. American cottontail rabbits are named for the white or light gray fur on the under-side of their tails. When a cottontail hops, its tail looks somewhat like a bouncing ball of white cotton.

Most rabbits live in a shallow hole called a form. Some rabbits live in a form throughout the year. Others, especially those of the north-ern United States and Canada, find a better protected home in winter. The winter den may be in a burrow, or under a pile of brush, rocks, or wood. Most rabbits do not dig their own burrows. They move into ones abandoned by such animals as woodchucks, badgers, prairie dogs, or skunks. Most rabbits live alone, but several may make dens in the same pile of brush.

Rabbits eat many plants. In spring and summer, their foods are green, leafy plants, including clover, grass, and weeds. In winter, rabbits eat twigs, bark, and the fruit of bushes and trees.

Enemies of rabbits include owls, hawks, mink, coyotes, foxes, weasels, and also dogs and cats.

BEYOND "THE END" . . .

LANGUAGE LINKS

Chrissy Cottontail shot "quick as a flash" through the blackberry bushes on Farmer John's farm. Expressions that cannot be understood or translated word for word, called idioms, give a language a special flavor. Another example is Chrissy sat very still because she knew if she moved, Ole Barney would be on her "like syrup on pancakes". Would it have been as interesting if the authors had written, "Chrissy Cottontail ran very fast through the blackberry bushes" and "Chrissy sat very still because she knew if she moved Barney would catch her"? Use of the idioms make the reading much more interesting!

Have you ever had a "crush on someone?" Have you ever "let the cat out of the bag?"

Ask your parents or grandparents to tell you idioms they have used. Write a short story using three of your favorite idioms.

CURRICULUM CONNECTIONS

Farmer John's daughter figured out that Chrissy Cottontail was a girl based on her sister, Amber, telling her that girl rabbits are larger than boys. Chrissy was larger than the other two rabbits, so she must be a girl!

Logic is reasoning or clear, sound thinking. Try some clear, sound thinking on these:

Solutions at end of unit.

1. In which year did Christmas Day and New Year's Day fall in the same year?
2. Everything Mr. Red owns is red, he lives in a red bungalow and his

chairs are red, his tables are red. His ceiling, walls, and floor are all red. All of his clothes are red. What color are his stairs?

3. Is it better to write a letter to Santa on an empty stomach or a full stomach?

4. You have a barrel, filled to the top with water, which weighs 150 pounds. What can you add to it to make it lighter?

Why is a hare not a rabbit? Tell how they are alike and different.

NUMBER OF CARROTS EATEN

Jack Cottontail   20
Mack Cottontail   10
Chrissy Cottontail   17

1. Who ate 17 carrots?
Mack or Chrissy
2. Who ate 10 carrots?
Jack or Mack
3. How many carrots did Jack eat?
10 or 20
4. How many carrots did Jack and Mack eat? 30 or 27
5. How many carrots did Jack and Chrissy eat? 27 or 37

THE BEST I CAN BE

Taking proper care of a pet teaches responsibility. If you have a pet rabbit, or hope to have one, look at this web site to learn DAILY RABBIT CARE: <www.showbunny.com/dailycare.htm>.

SOLUTIONS: 1. Every year at the beginning and end! 2. He doesn't have any stairs because he lives in a bungalow! 3. It's better to write it on paper! 4. Holes!